D1362988

THIS WALKER BOOK BELONGS TO:

_____

_____

_____

_____

For Sam White,
who is big AND brainy

L.A.

For David and Teresa

A.R.

First published 1995 by Walker Books Ltd
87 Vauxhall Walk, London SE11 5HJ

This edition published 2001

2 4 6 8 10 9 7 5 3

Text © 1995 Laurence Anholt
Illustrations © 1995 Arthur Robins

This book has been typeset in Journal.

Printed in Hong Kong

British Library Cataloguing in Publication Data
A catalogue record for this book is
available from the British Library.

ISBN 0-7445-7838-8

Knee-high Nigel

Written by Laurence Anholt
Illustrated by Arthur Robins

WALKER BOOKS
AND SUBSIDIARIES

LONDON • BOSTON • SYDNEY

There were once five giants who were
builders. Their names were Fee, Fi, Fo,
Fum and Nigel.

Fee

Fi

Together they built beautiful castles.

Fee, Fi, Fo and Fum were not very clever giants. They had never been to school and sometimes muddled their own names, but they were BIG and STRONG as every giant should be.

Nigel, on the other hand, had lots of bright ideas. He liked sums and drawing and inventing things; but the problem was – Nigel was far too small to be a proper giant.

In fact, he was so tiny

he had to bath in a boot

and sleep in a sock.

The other giants
called him
"Knee-high Nigel".

Every day Nigel sat indoors at a tiny
desk with a tiny cup of tea and drew
tiny but careful plans for enormous
and wonderful new castles.

And every day, whatever the weather,
Fee, Fi, Fo, and Fum would work outside,
pulling up trees and carrying boulders
to build the enormous and wonderful
castles Nigel had designed.
    They were so big they didn't need cranes.
    Nigel was brainy, the others were muscly
and everyone got along fine UNTIL...

One cold, wet Wednesday morning,
one of the big giants (it might have been
Fum) looked out at the muddy building
site and said,

"It's not fair."

Nigel was eating his breakfast (a whole
cornflake).

"What's not fair?" he said.

"We do all the hard work, rain or shine,
and you sit in 'ere not doin' nuffin'
nearly. It's not fair."

"Yeah!" said the others. "It's not fair."

"Right," said Nigel, reaching for his tiny
umbrella. "If that's how you feel, let's see
how you manage without me." And he
packed up all his tiny, careful drawings
and struggled out
into the rain.

The big giants didn't waste any time. They put a big advertisement in the newspaper.

Fee Fi Fo&Fum
WE WILL GET YOR
BILDIN DUN

Nigel wrote an advertisement too, but his was small and careful.

Knee-high Nigel
Qualified constructor of quite incredible quality castles
(By appointment to the Queen)

The big giants started work on a colossal concrete castle.

They built it by the sea because there was plenty of sand for the cement. They didn't have plans so they sort of made it up as they went along.

They put the roof on upside down

and forgot to
put in a door.

So it was probably
just as well ...

that the tide came in

and washed it all away.

Nigel was much smarter.
With tremendous care, he designed a
fabulous, luxurious castle, making sure
every detail was exactly right. He planned
a roof garden, an escalator, a fitted
kitchen with all kinds of gadgets.
Even a solar-heated jacuzzi.

"I will call it Sky-high Manor," he said.

Nigel was very pleased with himself –
until he started work. The trouble
was, Nigel couldn't lift
a single brick,

let alone
push a
wheelbarrow.

He couldn't mix the cement, and
when it started raining,
he slipped inside the
cement mixer,

completely spoiling his nice new suit.

"That's it,"
said Nigel.
"I've had
enough!"

Nigel walked wearily home and found the four big giants sitting on the step looking very gloomy.

"We're sorry, Nige," said Fee.

"We've been silly billies," said Fi.

"We don't need cranes..." said Fo.

"But we do need brains," said Fum.

"I'm sorry too, boys," said Nigel, brushing some cement from his shoe. "But look! I've got a brilliant idea for a new castle." And he pulled out the plans for Sky-high Manor.

"FANTASTIC!" said the big giants.

The next day, the big giants went outside to lay the foundations for Sky-high Manor. It was going to be their best castle yet.

Back at his desk, Nigel poured himself a tiny cup of tea and read through the advertisement he was writing –

Knee-high Nigel & Partners
(BIG AND BEAUTIFUL BUILDINGS)
"We've got muscle, we've got height,
and one of us is really bright."

"That's me!" said Knee-high Nigel.

LAURENCE ANHOLT says of **Knee-high Nigel**, "I stole the idea for this book and I hope the real Nigel won't mind. One day, when I was visiting a village primary school, I noticed a tiny boy who kept getting knocked down in the playground. 'That's little Nigel,' said the headmistress. 'Not much of an athlete.' That afternoon, the children and I thought up ideas for picture books; almost all the best ideas came from one person ... it was little Nigel, the tiny boy with a GIANT-sized imagination!"

Laurence Anholt met his wife, Catherine, when they were students. Since graduating, they have worked on numerous picture books together, including *Here Come the Babies, Kids, What I Like, What Makes Me Happy* and *Big Book of Families* for Walker. Laurence and Catherine live in Dorset, with their three children. Visit the Anholt website: www.anholt.co.uk

ARTHUR ROBINS says, "I had to keep in mind that Nigel is only knee high to Fee, Fi, Fo and Fum, and he is a giant – so they must be massive!" Arthur has illustrated numerous books, including the Walker picture books *Mission Ziffoid, The Magic Bicycle, The Teeny Tiny Woman* and *Little Rabbit Foo Foo*. He is married with two daughters and lives in Cranleigh, Surrey.

Laurence Anholt and Arthur Robins are the creators of the winner of the Smarties Prize Gold Award, *Seriously Silly Stories*.

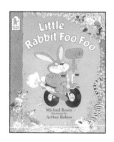
ISBN 0-7445-6945-1 (pb)

ISBN 0-7445-3651-0 (pb)

ISBN 0-7445-6067-5 (pb)

ISBN 0-7445-7729-2 (pb)